TIME'S WITNESS

Gareth Davies

We all have our time machines, don't we. Those that take us back are memories... And those that carry us forward, are dreams.

HG WELLS

CONTENTS

Title Page

Copyright

Epigraph

First Touch   1

First Awakening   5

Shifting Stones   8

The Quiet Future   11

Stone Memory   15

Vanished Stones   18

Age of Divergence   21

Lattice of Light   25

Silence of the Stars   28

Celestial Halo   30

Jewels of Life   32

Universal Silence   34

Broken Shells   36

Echoes of the Past   38

Quantum Frost   40

Dust to Dust   41

Rise of the Black Holes   43

Entropy Wins   45

Evaporation   46

The End of the Universe   47

The Last Laugh   50

Acknowledgement   55

About The Author   57

FIRST TOUCH

Carl never thought of himself as a man bound for adventure. His life was small and local, stitched together from the kind of routines that pass unnoticed until they're broken. He worked as a restorer of antique clocks. Tending to the delicate wheels and pendulums of centuries past and perhaps that was irony enough. A man who spent his days resurrecting timepieces would one day find himself cut loose from time entirely.

It began on a morning when the world was unusually still. The air carried the faint dampness of night rain, and a low mist coiled over the hedgerows. Carl had taken the path out of town, the one that skirted the abandoned railway cutting and led into the open fields along the valley, because something strange had been reported in the papers. A falling light, seen the night before, that villagers swore had landed somewhere in the meadows. Most dismissed it as a meteor but curiosity nagged at him like an itch.

The field he entered was churned with mud, the grass

pressed flat as if something immense had rolled and shifted upon it. But then he saw, at the far end where the mist clung thickest, stood an object.

It was not a stone, nor any familiar artifact of human making. It resembled a shell, long and slightly curved with a surface that shimmered iridescently like oil upon water. No marks of fire or impact scarred it and no trail showed its arrival. It seemed simply as though placed, as if the earth had grown it overnight.

Carl circled it cautiously, half expecting some other curious people to appear, but there was only the hush of the morning and the distant cries of crows. The surface was cool beneath his hand. Slick yet firm, like polished slate. His touch set off faint pulses of light beneath, as if the thing acknowledged him.

A seam appeared noiselessly and widened into a glowing opening. Carl should have fled. He knew that, even as his heart quickened. But the glow from within drew him forward, a soft warmth that felt more welcoming than threatening. His fingers, smeared with mud, brushed the edge of the aperture and it yielded.

Inside was no chamber of machines, no cockpit with levers or seats. It was smooth, rounded and alive with a light that shifted like liquid. He stepped across the threshold. The air within was different, thinner yet strangely invigorating. His breath felt lighter.

The opening sealed. Carl spun, but the seam had vanished as though it had never been. For a moment panic seized him but then the light intensified, forming streams that traced along the curved walls, converging above him. It was as though he stood within the heart of a great clock, not with cogs and gears, but with currents of luminous fluid. The patterns moved rhythmically, almost breathing.

Carl whispered to himself, "It's a machine." But it wasn't a machine that he could understand.

The floor shifted beneath his feet. Not dropping and not rising, but folding. He felt as though he had been turned inside-out without pain, his stomach lurching yet not sickened. His watch, the brass one he always carried, flickered and slowed. Its hands dragging as though thick syrup resisted them.

Time itself faltered.

He staggered and clutched at the wall. His fingertips sank slightly into it, like pressing into firm clay, though the surface sprang back instantly.

Then came the silence. Not the silence of a quiet morning, but a hollowing out, as if every ticking clock in the world had stopped at once. He realised with a chill that even his own heartbeat had gone soundless, though he felt it still beating.

In that silence, something pressed against his thoughts. Not a voice, not words, but a suggestion: "You may walk forward, if you choose."

Carl did not answer. Perhaps he could not. The sensation ebbed, and the chamber darkened. He lay down without meaning to, as though the floor itself shaped to cradle him. The air thickened like velvet around his skin.

Consciousness dissolved.

FIRST AWAKENING

10^1 Years

Carl woke to voices. He sat up, confused, expecting the cathedral-like space but found himself instead inside a tent of translucent polymer, strange apparatus glowing faintly about him. People stood nearby, their clothes unfamiliar. Metallic fabrics, smooth surfaces and with a faint sheen at their temples where devices were mounted.

"Good God! He's awake."

Carl blinked. The voice belonged to a young woman in a fitted grey tunic. Others clustered behind her, muttering in accents almost but not quite familiar. "Where am I?" Carl croaked.

"You're safe," the woman said quickly, though her eyes betrayed awe. "You were found inside the Artefact."

He glanced about. Through the translucent wall he

glimpsed the black curve of the object, still lodged in the earth. Lights and equipment bristled all around it.

"How long has it been?" he began. The woman hesitated. "Ten years. It's been ten years since you entered. We thought you were dead."

Ten years. Carl tried to grasp it. His parents, his friends, all of them. Ten years had passed and he had not aged a day. "Why?" he whispered.

"We don't know," she admitted. "The Artefact preserves you somehow" she continued "and now you've returned."

They peppered him with questions. What had he seen inside? What had it done to him? He could answer little. He had closed his eyes and then opened them again.

For several days they examined him, scanned him, tested his blood. When they found no harm, no change beyond what could be explained, they allowed him to walk outside.

But the world was changed, but not unrecognisably. Cars still rolled along roads, shops still sold bread and milk. Yet the tone was different. Drones hummed overhead, screens brighter and stranger adorned every shopfront and the very air felt taut with expectation. He felt himself a ghost. A man displaced, a decade missed.

Then, one morning, he was drawn back. The Artefact beckoned, silently. He did not resist.

SHIFTING STONES

3×10^1 Years

After thirty years, when Carl stepped out once more, the meadow was no longer wild with weeds. The grass had been cut clean, even manicured, like the lawn of a great estate. He blinked, looking towards the lane. Where there had once been a stony cart track, now lay tarmac, neat and dark, lined with white paint. A hum filled the air and in the distance a vehicle slid silently by, smooth and glassy, wheels hardly turning.

Carl walked the lane he had once known by heart, though it seemed to lead him somewhere different now. The cottages still stood, their honeyed stone glowing softly in the late light, but their faces had changed. Thatch was gone from many roofs, replaced by slate. Doors were painted in fresh colours. Gardens that once spilled wild with hollyhocks and lavender were neat, trimmed, almost curated.

He paused by the churchyard wall. The yew tree leaned heavier than before, its trunk broad and splitting. On the stones beneath, new names crowded the old. People he had known as children had already lived and died here. Their grandchildren played in the green, their voices bright and unfamiliar.

The Cotswold cottages, with their honey-coloured stone, still stood but their roofs were covered in panes of black glass that drank in the sun. Windows shimmered as if alive with faint colour, adjusting their transparency at will. The market square was bustling, though the market stalls were no longer sacks of potatoes or hand-carved tools but sleek kiosks displaying fruits that glowed faintly under embedded lights, fabrics that shimmered like water, devices of brushed steel and crystal.

Yet these people were still human, still dressed in coats and scarves, though cut in stranger lines. They spoke in accents Carl knew, although laced with clipped inflections he couldn't place.

One woman caught his eye, frowning. "Excuse me," Carl managed, his voice dry. "The baker, Thomas Avery, is he still here?"

The woman gave him a puzzled look. "There hasn't been a baker in these parts for decades. Where have you been hiding? One of those hermits up the hills?"

Carl stammered, "I was away. I..." He realised the absurdity of explanation. The woman shook her head, not unkindly. "Best get yourself to the centre, they'll help you there. You sound half-dazed." She gestured to the square.

Carl nodded numbly and drifted away before she could press further. It was then he realised: he had leapt again, not a decade, but more. The cottages were older but alive with new skin. The people knew nothing of the world he'd left. Thirty years had gone in the blink of his eye.

He stood in the square until dusk, watching the lights shimmer on, strange lanterns that glowed without flame. Children ran past him, laughing, tugging kites that hovered without string. Carl felt himself a ghost among them.

That night he returned to the meadow. The chamber waited silently, pulsing faintly. Patiently.

THE QUIET FUTURE

10^2 Years

C arl awoke again to silence.

The chamber dissolved and with it the village he had once known. He lay within a vessel of glass and pale metal, its edges humming with a pulse he did not understand. Beyond the transparent wall stretched a Cotswold valley, but not the one he remembered.

Honey stone cottages still nestled among the hills but many had been folded into structures of light and curve, their old bones absorbed into a fabric of glass and living green. Roads were gone, replaced by winding paths that glowed faintly beneath the grass. Above the rooftops, slender craft glided noiselessly, their reflections sliding across mirrored streams. The sky seemed clearer than he had ever known, almost sharpened by some hidden hand.

Carl rose, pressing to the glass. The fields were still patchworked with hedges, but threaded now with terraces that climbed into the air, gardens woven vertically into shining spires. The ancient hills endured, but they wore a strange new skin.

A figure entered the chamber. She was taller than him, with fine-boned features and eyes that seemed lit from within. Human still, but altered, refined.

"You are awake," she said, her voice calm, carrying an accent that curled strangely on the ear.

"Where am I?" Carl whispered.

"Still in your Cotswolds," she replied. "Though they are not as you knew them. The Pod is preserved among us as a mystery and you, Carl, are its Witness."

"Pod?" he repeated, the word foreign, though it was meant to name the very thing that held him. She tilted her head. "An artefact. There are several now. The others don't open. You're the only one who's come out."

Carl shivered. "You know of them? The thing in the meadow?"

Her eyes lit. "Yes. They arrived a hundred years ago. We've studied what we can. The others who entered never returned. But you, you've returned."

Carl's throat tightened. "But why me? Why is it doing this?"

The woman smiled faintly. "Why does anything? Perhaps you chose. Perhaps it chose you. But you must decide, do you stay with us or go back into the flow of time?"

Carl rose unsteadily. Through the glass walls he saw the towers rising, the gardens spiralling into the sky. It was marvellous. Terrifying. He had never felt so far from home.

He whispered, "I can't stop now."

The woman inclined her head. "Then you are a traveller of time, Carl Fletcher. The world will remember you."

Carl said nothing. He stared at his watch. It still marked the same frozen moment. Carl staggered. Everyone he had known was dead. The world had rebuilt itself, reshaped itself. He was a relic, a living fossil.

They called him the Witness. Scholars studied him, asking for stories of his time. Crowds came to see him, marvelling that a man from the past still walked among them.

But Carl knew, with a dread certainty, that he would not remain.

That night he returned once more to the alien

chamber. His hands shook but his heart pulled him forward. The chamber closed like a sigh, and silence enfolded him.

The Artefact waited.

STONE MEMORY

5×10^2 Years

The chamber held him again, dark and patient. He had begun to know its silences, the way it seemed not so much to sleep as to wait. When next it opened, Carl stepped into air that was not quite the air he remembered.

The Cotswolds remained, but transformed. The rolling hills were still green, yet the green shimmered, richer than any grass he had ever known, glowing faintly under a sun filtered by unseen veils. As he drew breath, he realised the air itself was changed — cleaner, almost sweet, carrying no trace of smoke or soot.

He walked forward, though the meadow was gone. In its place stood a plaza of translucent stone, veined with light that pulsed gently beneath his boots. At its centre, a fountain rose not of water but of mist shaped into patterns by invisible fields, spiralling like the petals of a flower.

The valley had become a vast arcology: a living city whose towers climbed higher than mountains, their sides covered in foliage that changed colour with the seasons in a single day. Above, delicate threads of silver traced the sky, carrying slow-moving platforms that glittered with tiny lights. Carl gaped, his heart pounding.

A figure approached him, tall, graceful, clad in robes that flowed like liquid silver. Their face was human but elongated, the eyes larger, the skin unblemished and faintly luminous.

"You are displaced," the figure said, their voice a harmony of tones as if more than one person spoke through them.

Carl swallowed. "I am from another time."

The being smiled gently. "Yes. We know of you. The Witness, from five hundred years ago. Your name is remembered in our chronicles. Some call you a legend. Few believed you would return."

Carl felt his knees weaken. "Remembered? I'm just a man."

The figure tilted their head. "Perhaps once. But through your leaps, you have become more. You walk when others only dream of walking. You are the witness of centuries."

Carl staggered to a bench, or something like a bench, a surface that rose softly to meet him. He pressed his face into his hands. "Everyone I knew. All gone, centuries ago!"

The figure seated themselves beside him. "Gone, yes, but not lost. Their traces remain, as do yours and you may go on, if you choose. The pod still answers to you."

Carl looked up sharply. "You know of it? You understand it?"

A faint smile. "We study it. We revere it. But we do not command it or understand it. You are its only constant."

Carl shivered. "Why me?" The figure's eyes shimmered. "Perhaps because you entered when none else dared. Many others tried but only you survive"

Carl said nothing more. That night he lay again in the pod's embrace, though the city's towers gleamed like stars above him, and he wondered if he was more prisoner than traveller.

VANISHED
STONES

10^3 Years

W hen next the chamber opened, he scarcely
recognised the world at all. The hills remained
only as memory, their outlines visible in the
contours of a vast, terraced structure that covered
the land like the hull of some sleeping colossus.
Above, the sky was not merely blue but streaked
with ribbons of shifting light, like aurora woven into
permanent fabric.

Carl stepped out onto a platform of glass that curved
endlessly into distance. Around him stood forms
that were human and not human — some tall and
willowy, some compact with gleaming implants of
metal and crystal. Others drifted without touching
the ground, their shapes blurred at the edges, as if
partly light themselves.

Then one approached, their voice resonating with warmth. "Carl Fletcher. The Witness."

He trembled. "How is it you know me still?"

The being's eyes glowed faintly. "Your name has travelled a thousand years. Time's Witness. You are the witness of the ages. You appear when we least expect, yet always when we most wish for memory of the past."

Carl shook his head. "But I wasn't meant for this. I stumbled in by chance."

The being raised a hand. "Yet here you are. Chance is often the face of purpose."

They gestured and Carl saw, spread across the valley, not cities but something greater. A living network, towers that grew like trees, their branches connected by spans of light. In the sky, vast shapes glided, larger than airships, glowing like slow comets.

"Is this England?" Carl whispered.

The being's smile was tinged with sorrow. "The name survives only in our records. The earth has changed and nations have dissolved. We are one people now, spread across many worlds. Earth, the Moon, Mars, Enceladus. Even some on Venus."

Carl's breath caught. "Many worlds?"

"Yes. Beyond the sky. Beyond the old boundaries."

Carl trembled. "Yet I remain the same."

The being regarded him steadily. "For now. But time will change you as it has changed us all. Already you are more legend than man. Will you continue?"

Carl closed his eyes. The thought of returning to the pod filled him with dread and wonder in equal measure. He could stop now. He could live among them, learn their ways, perhaps even find a place. Yet the chamber called to him still, as if promising vistas beyond imagining.

When he opened his eyes, he whispered: "I must go on."

The being inclined their head as though in benediction. "Then go, Witness. Carry our memory with you."

AGE OF DIVERGENCE

10^4 Years

C arl awoke to stars.

He drifted in a dome that opened onto the universe itself, with no barrier between him and infinity but a veil of crystal. Below stretched the Moon. Its surface a tapestry of ancient craters with the faint shimmer of domes scattered across its plains. Above him, the sky gleamed with constellations subtly altered by the slow hand of time.

Something or someone approached, fluid and luminous. A figure shaped like a human yet wrought of liquid metal and light. It moved with a grace beyond flesh, and when its eyes met his, they burned like white stars.

"Carl Fletcher. Witness." it said, and the sound was like music played on unseen strings. "You have returned."

His voice was rough with awe. "Returned? From where? How long?"

The being tilted its head, as though listening to echoes. "From the silence of the Artefact. Ten thousand years have passed since your first sleep."

Carl turned to the Earth. Blue, radiant, alive but distant. Different. He reached toward it, hand trembling against the glass.

"Ten thousand years" The words came out as a whisper. "Even earth no longer looks the same."

"Earth endures," the being replied, its tone both gentle and vast. "But it is no longer alone. Humanity has sown itself among the stars."

Carl's breath caught. "Then we made it? We survived?"

"We flourished," said the being. "Empires rose and fell, children of Earth built homes on other worlds. You are remembered, though not as you were. Stories linger. Fragments of myth and legend."

Carl pressed a hand to his chest. His body felt alien. Lighter, stronger, with his skin subtly altered. "The Artefact. It's changing me."

"Yes. It preserves. It prepares. You are its traveller."

"But why me?" His voice cracked with both fear and wonder. "I was no one. Just a man. A farmer's son."

The being's eyes glowed brighter and for a moment its voice harmonised into chords. "Perhaps because you entered. Perhaps because you dreamed. The Artefact does not explain itself, even to us."

Carl shuddered. He felt the pull returning. That inevitable tide drawing him back into the depths.

The being placed a hand of liquid metal on his shoulder, weightless yet steady. "Do not fear. Each awakening is not an ending but a step. You are witness to time itself."

Then, as before, the Artefact folded him away.

Ten years. A hundred. A thousand. Ten thousand. Each awakening was a window into a stranger age. Each return stripped away a layer of the man who had once known the quiet hills and fields of the Cotswolds.

Now he began to see his purpose. He was not merely surviving. He was witness. Passenger. Chosen not for power but for vision.

Deep within the Artefact, something vast and unknowable stirred. Not hostile, not kind, but intent. It was showing him the story of time itself, and he was both spectator and thread within its weave.

LATTICE OF LIGHT

5 x 10^4 Years

C arl awoke after fifty thousand years with the faintest shudder of the chamber, as though it had sighed him back into life. At once he knew something profound had shifted. His lungs drew air that was not quite air. Richer, warmer, laced with currents he could not name.

His eyes opened to brilliance and he flinched before realising that his vision had changed. Light no longer stabbed but unfolded. Every spectrum visible, colours that had no names sliding against each other in layered harmonies. He blinked, but the hues remained. The chamber had altered him.

He stepped out, and the ground was not earth. It was crystal, latticed, glowing faintly with inner fire, stretching to a horizon that had no curvature. Above him hung a star so vast it filled half the sky, its golden face haloed by immense, deliberate shadows.

The work of minds. At first Carl thought he was hallucinating but then recognition struck. This was a Dyson structure, the fabled sphere or shell of speculation, enclosing a star. Reality now before him. Humanity, or what followed it, had caught the sun in a net of industry, bending it to their will.

Figures moved across the lattice. They were not men and women, nor beasts, nor machines. Some were tall and transparent, refracting the starlight into prisms as they walked. Others rolled on wheels or hovered on unseen force, jointed. Limbs folding and unfolding like origami of steel. Still others were mere flakes of colour, darting across the lattice in pulses that his altered eyes began, slowly, to read as language.

One such crystalline figure turned toward him. Its body shone with inner seams of light. When it spoke, the sound came directly to his mind.

"Carl Fletcher. Witness."

The word struck him as both recognition and title. He tried to answer aloud. "Who are you?"

The figure's glow intensified, and though the sound of its words was like a thousand chimes, Carl understood. "We are many. Not human, yet born of them. This is fifty millennia since you last woke. Earth is memory. Humanity has scattered across the spiral arms. We diverge in form and thought. But you remain."

"I remain," Carl echoed, voice cracking. His hands trembled and only then did he notice they were not quite his hands. The skin was clear, faintly luminous, bones visible as lines of pale radiance. He flexed them, horrified and awed at once. "What has happened to me?"

"The chamber remakes you," said the figure. "It prepares you for what you will witness." Carl swallowed. "Why? Why me?"

The figure tilted its head, light scattering across its form. "Because you entered. Because you began. The chamber has its purpose. You are not random. You are chosen."

Carl wanted to protest. He had stumbled into the alien artifact by accident, curiosity and dread mingling, but the figure was already receding, its outline dissolving into the star's glow.

SILENCE OF
THE STARS

10^5 Years

The next awakening at one hundred thousand years came with silence so deep it felt like weight. Carl opened his eyes inside a chamber suspended in blackness. Beyond its clear walls he saw not one star but many, each surrounded by shimmering filaments. Swarms of constructs drifted like pollen grains, orbiting with silent precision. When the chamber opened, he stepped into vacuum and yet he breathed. The machine had remade him further. His skin sealed, luminous, his blood replaced by something finer.

Shapes approached but they were not shapes at all. They were patterns, interference in his sight, like aurora dancing across nothingness. He realised they were beings of data, projected directly into his mind. They spoke without mouths.

"You are the Witness."

That title again. Carl's heart hammered. "I am Carl Fletcher. I was a man."

"You are still a man," they replied. "But carried forward. Preserved against time. You walk where we cannot, from then into now. You bear what we forget."

Carl shivered. "Forget?"

"Memory frays. Even in the vastness of data, entropy gnaws. We lose our starting point. You are that beginning, walking among us. We keep the chamber safe because of you."

Carl wanted to ask again who had made the machine, why it compelled him, whether he could stop. But already the patterns were scattering, as though his presence was an event to be observed, not a dialogue to be maintained.

Alone once more, Carl returned to the chamber. It sealed and, yet again, time fell away.

CELESTIAL HALO

5×10^5 Years

A t half a million years he woke where no planet lay, only an artificial ring a billion kilometres wide, glittering with oceans and forests suspended in engineered gravity. A construct so vast it coiled around a star like a bracelet, its inner surface green with forests, blue with seas. He staggered as he emerged, the scale impossible to bear. Mountains arched upward, curving with the structure, until they met the distant horizon above his head.

His body was different again. His thoughts flickered in ways that startled him: images, equations, and words spilled across his mind without effort, as though knowledge had been sewn into him during sleep. His flesh was alive with embedded light, veins pulsing like circuitry. He reached for a leaf from a nearby tree and its genetic code whispered to him as naturally as scent.

A group approached. They looked human at first glance. They were tall, robed and graceful. But their eyes glowed faintly and their shadows detached from their bodies, moving independently like attendants. One of them bowed.

"You are the Witness. The one who remembers what we cannot." she said. Her voice was music, layered with harmonics that made Carl's bones vibrate. "You walk again."

Carl's throat tightened. "Do you know me?"

"We know of you. The chamber endures, passed from star to star, kept as relic and oracle. Each time it opens, you are within. You are continuity."

"I'm not..." Carl hesitated. "I'm not special. I didn't choose this."

The woman smiled, though her smile was tinged with sorrow. "Choice is seldom the root of destiny."

Carl almost wept at her words. He wanted home, yet home was now five hundred thousand years gone. He had no one, nothing. And yet, in their eyes, he mattered.

JEWELS OF LIFE

10^6 Years

At last, after a million years, the chamber stirred once more. Carl opened his eyes upon a galaxy remade. Threads of power stitched the void, luminous arteries running from star to star. Dyson shells gleamed like jewels, hundreds of them, while vast fleets of thought and light drifted across the dark. He stood within a sanctuary, itself an artefact the size of a moon, and beyond its walls the galaxy glowed with deliberate fire.

His body, no, his being, was something new. He was form and data interlaced. He could step with feet yet also drift on currents of thought. He touched his chest and felt both flesh and code.

The chamber opened, and beings of impossible complexity gathered. Some were rivers of plasma, others lattices of machines the size of cathedrals, yet they all addressed him with one voice:

"You are the Witness."

Carl raised his altered hands. "Why? Why do you keep me? Why do you move me, shape me, stretch me through time?"

A silence fell. Then a single answer.

"Because the chamber wills it.

He felt it then. Not words, not reason but intention. The machine was not passive. It had guided him, deliberately, across epochs. It wanted him to see, to carry, to remember. He was not merely a man. He was the story.

But at a million years, staring into the galaxy's splendour, Carl felt something colder too: loneliness sharper than ever. He was the witness, yes. But he was also the last man, stretched across aeons with no place to rest.

UNIVERSAL
SILENCE

10^7 Years

After ten million years Carl awoke, though the word no longer carried its old meaning. The chamber stirred him into awareness, piecing his mind back together from whatever substrate it had become. His body was not flesh now, it had been remade into light woven within a lattice, a figure of radiant filigree. He was both solid and transparent, a walking contradiction.

The sky that greeted him was not Earth's, nor any he remembered from earlier awakenings. It was a whirlpool of stars, vast arms tangled, colliding galaxies painting the void with ribbons of gas. A billion suns blazed together, each circled by a corona of industry, but the sheer density of light overwhelmed him. His new senses filtered it, dimming brilliance into something he could bear.

For the first time in countless ages, no voices greeted him. No crystalline figure, no chorus of minds, no delicate bow. He was alone on a terrace of diamond rock, staring at a galactic merger that spanned the heavens.

"Hello?" His voice rang strangely, as if spoken into himself. "Is anyone there?"

Only silence.

He wandered, though the surface was featureless. He realised, slowly, that perhaps this was the point. The chamber had placed him not among people but among ruins. A witness to grandeur and collapse alike. The alien artifact, inscrutable as ever, was curating his journey.

BROKEN SHELLS

5×10^7 Years

Carl's next awareness came after fifty million years upon a dying sky. Stars burned red, swollen, their light heavy. Dyson shells lay cracked, fleets abandoned, worlds drifting without orbit. He stood in a chamber that had been carried far from any sun, hanging in the dark between systems.

His body had been altered again, no longer radiant lattice but something simpler, denser, a mind condensed into a single, glowing node that could drift through void without loss. He felt himself both more fragile and more eternal.

He reached out but nothing answered. Civilisations had passed in the blink of his sleep. He had missed their rise, their decline, their last spark. Whole histories extinguished in silence.

"I wasn't meant to be this alone," he whispered. The

chamber offered no reply.

ECHOES OF
THE PAST

10^8 Years

Stirring once again, he floated above a cold, dim star. After a hundred million years, its light was faint, its heat minimal. Around it drifted husks of great machines. Their forms worn down by time, their purpose forgotten. The galaxy itself had thinned and its spiral arms were smeared into clouds.

A voice touched him then, faint as a memory. "Witness..."

He turned, searching. A figure coalesced from motes of dust and magnetic flux. Not truly alive but a recorded echo.

"You still endure," it said. Its tone was tired, fragmented. "We do not." Carl reached for it, though his hands were little more than light. "Who were you?"

"Children of children of humankind. We lasted long but time wins. Time always wins."

The figure faded, leaving him staring into the cold.

QUANTUM FROST

5 x 10^8 Years

A wakening after five hundred million years was torment. Again, the chamber remade him into a form fit for survival. He was no longer recognisably human. His mind existed as distributed pulses of quantum frost across a shell of dark matter. He felt himself stretched and fractured, yet whole in ways he could scarcely understand.

The galaxy was unrecognisable. Its core was swollen with mergers, stars torn apart, black holes multiplying. Between his blinks of existence, civilisations had risen and fallen like sparks. He began to measure history in their absences.

At times he wept, or tried to. His new body had no tears.

DUST TO DUST

10^9 Years

When next he knew himself, a billion years later, there was almost nothing left of his home galaxy. The stars were sparse, red embers dwindling in black seas. The great works were gone. The Dyson shells and the ringworlds were dust and silence reigned.

Carl stood, though standing was only a metaphor now, upon the rim of a dead world. He looked up into the night and saw emptiness. Between his last awakening and now, entire galaxies had guttered out.

The chamber whispered within him, not words but intent. "Witness, still."

His voice echoed thinly in the barren air. "Why? There's nothing left."

But he knew, deep down, that there was always something more waiting beyond what could be measured. Entropy might roll forward like an endless tide, washing away the structures of stars and minds alike, yet he could not bring himself to believe it was the only destiny. A tide was powerful, yes, but even the strongest current could shift, could be turned by a change in the wind or the shape of the shore. Probability was not certainty and chance still left space for wonder.

Carl, the Witness, raised his head to the dwindling stars. He had carried memory from the Cotswolds to the edge of cosmic night. He had no choice but to continue.

RISE OF THE BLACK HOLES

10^{10} Years

After ten billion years, the chamber did not so much awaken Carl as re-assemble him from silence. His mind was a faint persistence, stretched thinner than gossamer threads across the aeons. Each interval was so vast that galaxies themselves had flickered out between his thoughts.

His body, if it could still be called that, no longer resembled anything earthly. It was an architecture of probabilities, a web of low-energy quantum states stabilised by the alien machine. He was a pattern more than a person, yet when awareness returned, he was still Carl. Still the Witness.

The sky was sparse. The familiar great spirals were gone, merged into bloated ellipticals. Stars burned cooler, redder, fewer. Black holes prowled, swallowing what remained. Carl stood, or existed, beside one such abyss, feeling its slow inhalation of the universe.

No voices greeted him. No echoes remained of humankind or its descendants. The chamber had carried him faithfully through time, but the pageant was almost finished.

ENTROPY WINS

10^{12} Years

A trillion years later, time became uncountable. Carl's awakenings were now flickers, motes of memory in an endless dark. He saw the last star burn out in a distant galaxy, its embers collapsing into a white dwarf, then into nothing.

The universe slowly, oh so slowly, dimmed. Heat and cold joined forces into thermal equilibrium. Motion slowed. All gradients flattened into sameness. Entropy, the great leveller, had won.

And yet Carl remained.

Suspended in the time, he persisted where nothing else did. Why had it chosen him? What purpose could possibly remain at the end of time? He tried to reason, but reasoning itself faltered, for there was almost no information left to grasp.

EVAPORATION

10^{40} Years

Only black holes were left. With nothing to feed on they slowly evaporated into pure radiation. Carl drifted through one such end, watching it shrink to nothing.

The last titans of creation dissolved into formless energy, thinly smeared across infinity.

Still, he endured.

THE END OF
THE UNIVERSE

10^{100} Years

By ten thousand trillion trillion trillion trillion trillion trillion trillion trillion years, the black holes were gone. All but one. The universe was a thin soup of photons and faint particles, spread so evenly that no structure remained. Entropy was the highest it could possibly be.

Carl floated in the void, alone, a single thread of identity stitched through nothingness. He was not awake in the human sense, there was no body to anchor him, but something still maintained his continuity. Ego persisted, fragile and stubborn, like a candle in a place without air.

Carl awoke into silence deeper than silence. An absence so total it pressed upon his thoughts like a weight. At first, he assumed the chamber had failed, that its alien machinery had finally ground to a halt. But then, slowly, he realised it was not the chamber that had fallen quiet. There was no chamber, it was the universe itself.

He stretched his senses, such as they had become, into the dark. Where once he had awakened to stars, or nebulae, or the shimmering outlines of vast constructions wrought by hands he could no longer quite call human, now there was almost nothing. Almost. The faintest drizzle of photons, the long tail of decaying light, drifted like embers from a fire so long extinguished that its ashes had blown to the edge of forever.

Carl whispered into the void, not with lips, but with that resilient thread of thought the machine kept burning.

"I am still here."

There was no chamber now. His body, if such it could be called, perhaps his essence, was no longer flesh, nor even the crystalline latticework he had once been remade into. It was a pattern of persistence, an organisation of information and energy carefully insulated from the ravages of entropy.

He had been the Witness of ages. Now he was the Witness of endings.

The scale of time defied comprehension. Carl drifted through aeons where nothing changed at all. Then, without warning, a last black hole, once a monster at the heart of a galaxy, gave its final sigh, glowing with its last whisper of Hawking radiation before vanishing into nothingness. The event came and went in a blink, though that blink spanned millions of years.

He mourned it, absurd though the act was. Not the hole itself, an object without sympathy or malice, but the idea that yet another chapter of existence had closed. How many had he seen close now? Civilisations rose and burned between his awakenings like sparks on a log. Stars flared, dimmed, died. Structures of unimaginable scale once surrounded him; now their remnants cooled into silence.

And still he remained.

THE LAST LAUGH

10$^\infty$

There were no voices to greet him anymore. No figures who would point and murmur that the Witness has returned. He was alone but not without a purpose. For though the universe seemed flat and featureless, he began to notice something strange. Once in a span so long it might as well have been forever, a flicker. A reversal of entropy, which normally always increased, seemed for a heartbeat to stumble. A patch of order bloomed, molecules aligning, patterns forming spontaneously in the dark before dissolving back into chaos.

Carl fixed upon it. His thoughts, sharpened across eternity, clung to the anomaly. Can it be possible? It isn't impossible. That is enough.

He had been the witness to growth, to decline, to the long dwindling dusk. Yet something in him resisted the idea that his journey ended here, floating in nothingness, waiting for the last ember to fade.

"I am still here." he repeated and the words rang in the dark as if testing the silence for cracks. The universe itself seemed to shiver.

The cracks widened. Not literal fissures in space, but subtle undulations in the vacuum energy, the nothing beneath reality. Carl felt them not with sight, nor with hearing, but with the core of himself as though his very persistence was tugged by invisible tides.

The quantum foam rippled. He had heard of it, long ago, in his first lifetime. Even in vacuum, nothingness seethed with uncertainty, particles popping in and out of existence. Back then, it was only a theory. Now, stretched beyond comprehension, he felt it as fact.

Tiny flashes stirred. Where once they winked out again without effect, now some lingered, clumping, folding together instead of cancelling out. Energy thickened, improbably, impossibly, against the weight of entropy.

Carl leaned, though there was no body to lean with, toward the tremor. "So this is it.", he thought. "Not an end, but a turn of the cycle."

The clumps condensed. The ripples deepened then, without hesitation, they snapped into a singularity. Not a metaphor, not an abstraction, but an actual point in which all the budding energy of a newborn cosmos gathered. It pulsed like a heartbeat, though it had no rhythm, waiting.

Aeons of time, yet no time at all, passed and he shed even the last pretence of form, until he was little more than an awareness poised against infinity. He understood, in a way words could never capture, that this was not chance. The artifact had carried him here for this. To see, to stand at the edge, to bear witness and perhaps more.

Carl hovered at the boundary of decision. He was, at the last, still human enough to crave meaning. To ask whether his being here mattered. Was he only watching, or was he expected to act?

The singularity trembled, as though it too were waiting.

He recalled his earliest life, his first days in the chamber, when he was simply Carl, a man startled into wonder. He remembered the landscapes of the Cotswolds, the first modern towns he walked through as a stranger in his own land. He remembered the voice of a girl who once pointed to him and whispered, the Witness. All of it was still within him, threaded through uncountable transformations.

He lifted the echo of a hand and with it, he made the most human gesture he knew.

He snapped his fingers.

The singularity broke. A brilliance surged outward, not light but the very seed of light. Space unfolded like a sail, time stretched like fresh cloth, energy burst and boiled, filling the void with heat and fire and law. The Big Bang.

Carl laughed, and the cosmos shivered at the sound that was not sound. Motes of his being, luminous and trembling, flowed outward like sparks from a primordial fire. They danced along the void, weaving through the emptiness, stirring the currents of the newborn universe. Where they swirled, eddies formed, folding space and time into patterns of possibility.

Gravity bowed to the impulse of his mirth, matter coalesced and from the ripples of his joy, the first seeds of stars, of galaxies, of worlds were sown. Each pulse of his laughter was a hymn, each shimmer a command: let there be shape, let there be light. In that instant, Carl was not merely alive. He was creator, witness, and instrument all at once and the universe itself had become his echo.

"I was the Witness at the end. Now I am the seed at the beginning."

Carl's essence scattered with the ripples of his laughter. He felt himself woven into the fabric of the nascent universe in the particles, in the forces, in the breath of expansion.

The universe unfurled, fresh and unmarked. Carl's story ended as it began, not with an ending at all, but yet another beginning.

Perhaps he would return, though by then there would be no memory of having left. Perhaps he already had.

ACKNOWLEDGEMENT

This book has been kicking about in my thoughts for many years, with the occasional words and sections committed to writing from time to time. With the advent of AI writing tools like ChatGPT, it is finally possible to fully realise my ambitions and actually complete a story.

As my long-suffering wife, Tina, has known for years, I am incapable of doing something new without fully comprehending it. Always asking why, or what if. This story and others have grown from those questions.

ABOUT THE AUTHOR

Gareth Davies

Gareth Davies is an electronics and software engineer who has been designing and building computers, computer chips, and educational robots since the 1970s. He runs 4tronix, a company that has created and sold more than 200,000 robots worldwide since 2009. He has a strong interest in fundamental physics, cosmology, astronomy, mathematics and a variety of other areas.

Gareth also writes science fiction that explores the strange edges of physics, philosophy, and the nature of reality. His books, including Time's Witness, A Room with a Skew, Spacetime Oddities, and Sparks to Quarks, invite readers to think differently about time, space, and the universe we inhabit.

Rather than focusing on conflict or dystopia, Gareth's stories are driven by curiosity and imagination with the aim of making complex ideas accessible and sparking wonder in readers of all ages.

Printed in Dunstable, United Kingdom